HAUNTED BUNGALOW

WHAT THE MYSTERY IS ??

MUDLIYAR UDAY KUMAR

Haunted Bungalow

Once upon a time there was a haunted bungalow where the ghost use to kill everyone by calling them inside .

Anil who was a boy of 20 years old . He used to love to see the horror pictures and videos on you tube . One day he told to his friends that

Anil : Friends I want to see the real ghost do you know any haunted and horror place where I can experience real ghost.

Friend Sham : Yes , Just a 7 km faraway one haunted bungalow is there , where anybody goes there doesn't return back . 2 days before Ramu uncle who used to sell ice-creams he went inside by mistake and he never came back .

Anil : Friends today we will go inside that bungalow and see what exactly happens , are you ready ?

Friend Vishnu : Hey sham why you told him about that bungalow ? You didn't know that he is very interested in such things .

Anil : Let it be I will only go there and come back again here .

All friends : No Anil it is very dangerous if you will go and never come back then ??

Anil : We will see at that time . Bye

[By telling "bye" he went to his home]

[At Home]

Now Anil had his dinner at 9.00 PM night and slept at 9.30 . Before sleeping he put the alarm of 2.55 AM means midnight . His Mother saw that and asked " Why you kept this alarm very early ??

Anil replied " Mom , I have to go to our aunt,s home so that's why.

Anil told lies because if he will tell the truth than his mother will never let him to go there .

[1st time]

Anil didn't know this , one day Ramu uncle who was fully drank he was just walking from the bungalow . He noticed that when he passed from the bungalows gate the cool air comes when he moved away he wanted to experience the cool air again so he stood near the gate . When he turned back and stand again his eagerness was increasing and to go inside . When he put the one leg on land cool air was blowing . Suddenly anybody came and touched his shoulder ,when he turned back to see who was it there was nobody at his back . But when he turned front near the gate he saw lady whose leg was little bit zig zag and that lady has a baby boy . She was asking him to leave her inside the bungalow . The ghost told that " Please leave me inside the bungalow I will give you 10,000 rupees . Due to his greediness he took that lady and leave her inside the bungalow and he asked to that lady that " Madam," you told that if I will leave you inside the house than you will give me 10,000 rupees" . Then where is my 10,000 rupees

Then the lady replied " which 10,000 rupees you want ??

Ramu Uncle : Why you are pranking me give my 10,000 rupees or I shall complaint to police .

[After telling this he removed his phone]

[That ghost took his phone]

Now that man was very angry and started shouting that " you told know I will give you 10,000 rupees why you not gave me ??

Ghost replied : Once you see my face and tell again .

Ramu uncle was shocked when he saw that

ghost face and ran away from there when he reached near the gate the gate was suddenly closed Ramu did not understand any thing because he was drunk . He tried to open and escape from that gate but he was unsuccessful . The ghost came near him and took one sharp sword and killed him as she was hungry and angry both . She ate Ramu uncle's half kidney half lungs and throwed him away from that bungalow near the gate . At morning his full body was covered with flies and some dog was biting and eating his body . Now all those who came near that place was shocked and called Police and police called ambulance . Police didn't take action. They thought that , " he will be drunk and hitted by a car on the street and may the street dogs would have bitted .

2nd time

A business man saw that house and visited inside that house . Now the ghost changed its getup and became as an watchman . When the business man entered suddenly he talked to the watchman .

Business man : Is this house for sale ??

Watchman : Yes sir this house is for sale .

Business man : Can I and my body guards go and see that bungalow from inside??

Watchman : Yes sir

[After , that business man and his guards went inside the bungalow . Suddenly one , one guards were started disappearing and in last 1 body guard was left and the business man . Now the watchman came and asked .

Watchman the ghost : What happened sir you are afraid ?

Business man : what is going on ??

[Now the watchman turned into ghost and came near them]

After seeing this they shooted that ghost by gun and started running from that place . Again same thing has happened . The ghost came closed the door and killed them . At morning again police came and called ambulance The business man escaped from there . Now there were confused that yesterday a man died today also group of associates are died . They taught that " when the group of associates would be entered the other associates who saw them they would have killed and took the revenge of them . This case was filed as a revenge case .

3rd Time

A gang of thiefs came there to keep there stollen things. Now the ghost was again in a watchman getup . Gang of thieves : Hey watchman can you give this bungalow we will give you 1,00,000 rupees ??

Watchman : Yes ,

Gang of thieves : Can you show us interior part of the bungalow .

Watchman : Yes

[Now the ghost uses that trick again]

One by one thieves started disappearing now the thieves gang leader Mr. Damodar was left .He tried to run from there but he was unsuccessful . The ghost again closed the gate and came to kill . When Damodar saw her face he told " Leave me , Anjali please forgive me .

Ghost : At that time I requested you, but you killed me . After telling this ,the ghost killed Damodar and at the next morning near that bungalow gate, his body was lying . Again Police came, called Ambulance and their family members were crying and again the police got confused .

[Anil didn't know this all things .

Now the Alarm of 2.59 AM rang . Anil got up ,he took his sweater and ran near the bungalow.

Before this ,why the ghost is killing all them ? Would the ghost will kill Anil and what

Anil will do ?? You will understand

Now Anil went inside the house . He noticed that the bungalow temperature was very low and the gate was closed . Anil was excited that what will exactly happen next , when he entered inside the bungalow and stand in a hall ,he heard that anybody is coming near him . So he hided behind a table . He saw that a women who's face was very scary . He was very afraid by seeing this . Now the ghost saw that Anil is hiding behind the table . Anjali the ghost went near him . But she was not able to do him . Before she do anything Anil ran away from that place and reached on a kitchen and hided over their . However that ghost saw him and now Anil was trying to escape from there so he jumped from an window and reached down . Now time is 5.30 AM .

[Now in home]

Anil,s mother with doubt she called Anil,s aunt . She recieved the phone .

Anil mom Reema: Hi Shalu , Sorry for disturbing you, Is my son is there at your home??

Shalni Aunty : No Reema what happened ??

Mom Reema : He told me that ,he is coming to your house and now you are telling that he not came where he could have go ??

Shalni Aunty : Call his friends and ask them about it .

Mom Reema : Good idea . Bye and sorry for disturbing you

Shalni Aunty : Ok bye .

[Then now Anil,s mother started calling Anil,s friends .

One of them said that

Friend Golu : Aunty , He might went to the haunted bungalow . Because he was asking from tody morning that anybody knows any haunted bangalow . Then his friend suggested that bungalow .

Anil,s Mom : Where is the bungalow ?

Friend Golu : Just 1 km away .

Anil,s Mom : Oh that Anjali,s house which is now haunted .

Friend Golu : Yes aunty .

Anil,s Mom : Thank you so much beta .

[After telling this she phone called Anil]

But due to some network issues the call no went to him . Anil jumped down but he was not able to go out . The ghost came near him to kill him . But something happens suddenly whenever she touches him . Now the Ghost remembered that what Baba has told to her before dying .

[Flashback]

One day Anjalis family baba came who knows all the background of her family he told that , " Anjali you are going to die but before your brother is going to die and after 2 months you are going to die .

Anjali with shock expressions : What ! Baba what are you telling really ??

Baba : Yes my child . As I said you , your brother is going to die after 1 month .

[When Anjali,s Brother Sham heard this he went to Baba and said]

Sham : I know why this Baba is telling like this . First he will take money and with that money he enjoy,s drinking alcohal at night .

Anjali : Brother please stop it ! What you know about this Baba ??

Sham : Nothing , But I know,he will do this .

Anjali : . Baba now my marraige is going to be held.

Baba : Only god knows all thing ,now I am going bye ! But when you will die and become a ghost you will be needed a good person body .

Anjali was upset .

[After 29 Days passed]

Now marriage function was going on there

After 2 years she died . How she died , will you explain?. Her brother was a leader of a village . Due to some jealous people he was killed .

[Anjali and Anil discussion]

Anjali : Can I go inside your body ?

Anil : Mam , My opinion is yes . Because I always stay close to Justice .

Anjali : Ok .

Anil : Mam why you want to come inside me ?

Anjali : I want to take some revenge .

Anil : If you will take the revenge , than the police will catch me only .

Anjali : Don,t take tension I am there .

Anil : And one more thing . If your work is finished than you should go out of my body and also from this bungalow . Ok ??

Anjali : Ok .

[Now she entered in his body]

[Now village people came near the bungalow's gate and shouted " Anil dont be afraid , we are there . They were holding broom and chappals .]

Anil,s body was now full of power .

[Now he shouted loudly]

After sometimes he opened the gate . The village people was suprised .

Anil,s Mother hugged him .

Anil,s Mother slapped him .

Anil,s Mother : Hey ! You don't have sense ??

Anil : Why mom ??

Anil's Mom : You don't know , that this house is haunted ??

Anil : No mom , I thought the people were telling lies and making us fool but when I entered this house I came to know it .

Village People : Reema let's go from here . Afterwards talk with your son .

Anil mom Reema : Ok .

[Night 3 .00 "o" clock .]

The ghost was activated inside Anil .

After this it went to Inspector Pradeep . All were sleeping in the station , because it was midnight . The ghost was crying outside the police station . Saying that " My baby has been kidnaped "

Now the dogs were also barking at the ghost .

[This sound was disturbing to all polices who were sleeping inside the police station .]

One of the constable went outside and saw . He was totally shocked when he saw the lady in white saree with bleeding eyes . He felt afraid and fell down .

Now the Inspector also came out . He also saw the lady crying , he also felt shocked .

Inspector : Why you are crying ??

[But there was no response from that lady]

Lady : I want something to eat .

Inspector : What ??

Lady : I want your kidney .

[After telling this she took her knife and killed the police]

[Next morning]

This news reached to the media however , and the news became viral .

[Next night]

The ghost was activated again in Anil,s body and went to the Grampanchayat leader house . Now who is the leader of the village .

His name is Rajshekar .

The ghost went inside the Rajshekar house

and killed him .

[Next Morning]

This news also became viral .

[Next night]

His family members saw that Anil is going out , so his mother slapped him and brought inside .

His face was normal .

Mother : You don't have sense ??

Anil : Yes mom ...

Mother : What !

Anil: I don't know what is happening to me at night .

Mother : Why ??

Anil : Yes mom .

[So now he told all things]

Mother : I can understand the ghost feeling's but why the ghost choosed you .

Anil : Mom , I only gave the permission .

Mother : But .

[Suddenly the ghost came inside him]

Anjali ghost : As I know that you are the mom of Anil .

I also see you as a mother .

Mother of Anil : So why you entered to my son,s body ??

Anjali : I want to take some revenges .

Mother of Anil : Why ?? It means you only killed inspector and the village leader ??

Anjali : Yes .

Mother of Anil : Why ??

Anjali : 7 years before , my brother Sham was the leader of the village . Mr.Rajshekhar was the Grampanchayat leader . The police was the Inspector only . One day a company M.d came here to build his company, due to some issues . He was against the law . My brother came to know it , so he rejected the deal . After some days passed . He was fixing my marraige . Before this , when I was small my mother and father died . My brother took my care . When his age was 13 instead of studying he used to work in an loom factory . However he only took my care .

With love and care he fixed my marraige spending all his money on it .

The Grampanchayat leader , company Md and the police planned to kill my brother .

Granpanchayat Leader : How we should capture that place ??

Police Inspector : No idea .

Company M.D Rahul : I have an Idea .

Grampanchayat leader name is Rajshekhar and Inspector name is Mr. Madhav Singh .

Both : What's the idea ??

Rahul : There is no way instead , of killing Sham .

Both : What !! [With shock expression]

Rahul : Yes , Tomorrow Sham and Anjali will go to take the gold , so at that time we will send a truck and accident them .

Both : Idea is good , but will it happen ??

Rahul : We will make it happen .

[As their Idea was not success because , they didn't went to buy any jewellery . They had bought at morning only ,]

Rahul : Shit !

Both : As we asked you at first that , it will happen ??

Rahul : So what ??

Both : then ??

Rahul : I have an Idea .

Grampanchayat leader and inspector : What is the idea ??

Rahul : As , tomorrow Anjali's marriage is there .

They both replied : Yes .

Rahul : First make sure that Anjali and Sham is going in same car.

[They however came to know that Sham and Arjun is going at same car]

Inspector : Rahul sir they both are going in same car .

Rahul : Listen , the plan is same we will send the truck and accident them .

Both : But , what's the profit to us ??

Rahul : As I told you that , Inspector will get

the money upto 35 lakhs and Grampanchayat leader will became as the leader of this village .

Both excepted the deal .

[Now according to their plan they did it .]

[The truck crashed the car]

Ambulance came to take both of them .

[In hospital]

Doctor : Anjali there is nothing to you . But .....

Anjali : What happened to my brother ??

Doctor : Sorry , We can't save your brother .

Anjali : Doctor what you are saying !!

Doctor : Sorry we are helpless .

[Anjali was crying loudly]

She went to flashback that how her brother took the care of her .

Anjali's Husband : Don't cry Anjali .

Anjali : What you are saying .

Anjali's Husband : I can understand your feeling's but .

[After few hours , they did the formalities for that body .]

One day Anjali and his husband went to hospital . The doctor checked her and replied " Anjali , there is a good news ."

Anjali : What is that doctor ??

Doctor : You are Pregnant .

[After listening it she was very happy]

[Few days later]

Grampanchayat leader , Business man and Inspector came to Anjali ,s house .

They knocked the door .

Anjali opened the door and was surprised , that they all came to Anjali,s house .

Anjali welcomed them .

Anjali,s husband came down to see that who has came .

[Ram was Anjali,s husband name .]

Ram : Anjali , who are they ?

Anjali : They are my village main people . Meet him his name Rajshekhar . He is our village Grampanchayat leader .

Ram : Hi [Shaked hands]

Anjali : Raj he is inspector name is M.r Madhav Singh .

Ram : Hi !sir [Shaked hands]

Anjali : Rajshekhar sir ,who is this man ??

Rajshekhar : He is a business man name Rahul . He wanted to make a company in middle of the village .

Anjali : So why he came here ??

Rajshekhar : We want your permission . Because , after your brother you are the head of our village that's we are asking your permission .

Anjali : Because of that , what profit will the village people get ?

Rahul : All village people will get a chance to work there .

Anjali : Oh , Ok .

Rajshekhar : What's your decision Anjali ??

Anjali : You can built it .

Rajshekhar : Ok .

Anjali : Actually , I wanted to tell you one thing uncle .

Anjali :: My brother told , that " This factory building is against the law .

Rajshekhar : First it was . But now we improved it .

Anjali : I have decided one thing that " I will give my village ,s head posting to you "

Rajshekhar : Why ??

Anjali : Because from Mumbai to our village I can't come .

Rajshekhar : Why Anjali ??

Anjali : Because , If I will come there than nobody is there for me . First my brother was there but , now nobody is there .

Rajshekhar : I can understand your felling's .

Anjali : Ok uncle . Tomorrow bring the form that contains " I promise you / I will give you my C.M post of village .

Rajshekhar : Ok .

[Night time]

[In an hotel]

Business man Rahul : I thought that , you only to clear the misunderstand of people . But today I know that you can also act .

Rajshekhar : This was nothing

Inspector : Yes .

[At Anjali,s home]

Anjali,s Husband Ram : Anjali if I will tell you one thing than you will not feel bad .

Anjali : First you tell what the thing is .

Ram : I have an doubt on Rajshekar sir .

Anjali : What's the doubt is ??

Ram : He is said that " We are building a factory in middle of village ."

Anjali : Yes .

Ram : I think it is wrong . Because building a factory in middle of village that also gas factory it is not good .

Anjali : Why ??

Ram : Because , by mistake some gas got leak it can be harmful for people .

Anjali : I believe Uncle . It will not happen .

Ram : Ok .

[At Morning]

Rajshekhar , Business man and Inspector at Anjali,s home with an Advocate .

Rajshekhar : Anjali you have to read the agreement and sign their .

Anjali : What is there in that agreement ??

Advocate : Anjali , By signing the agreement you agree that you are giving your village C.M seat to M.r Rajshekhar and you will never ask it return .

Anjali : Ok sir .

[Anjali signed the agreement and gave it to the advocate]

After this they went to court . Chief Justice asked some questions related to the agreement . Anjali answered and agreed for that .

[2 Days passed]

[In Village]

Rajshekhar announced that " From now I am your leader . Anjali gave the seat to me . By seeing the agreement you can understand it "

[Village people also agreed it . They believed that , what decision Anjali take it will be right .]

[After 2 years]

Anjali planned to visit the village and see the factory .

The village was totally in bad condition .

Anjali asked one of the women about it .

Women : Before 2 years collected the money from village people for building the factory.

Anjali : I have given him all the money to build factory . But why he collected the money from village people .

Women : After that he started collecting monthly , monthly 1000 rupees from every people . He gave a chance to the village people to work . He gave salary to the people . He gave per person 1000 rupees salary . After that one of the man came to know that , the money which he collects he give that money back to people in form of salary . After the village people came to know then they did the strike . After that he stopped collecting 1000 rupees and started giving the people 1200 rupees . The people were little bit happy . After that he started selling the Oxygen tank to foreign at higher price . Then too he does not increased our salary . One of the boy saw that , they use many chemical that cost less but it is harmful . He was caught by Rajshekhar and was killed . After that he stopped it . He started to make Injections which is bad for health . That also we came to know . But He threated us that " If you all people will tell to police than he will release the bad gas .

Anjali : This much is happened . The matter is very serious . I have to talk .

[So she went inside factory alone]

Asked about it . She phone called police but , the call was cut by Rahul . They all killed Anjali . Even Inspector also was there with them . After killing Anjali . They gave complaint on police that Anjali,s husband Ram killed her . Now also he is in jail .

[This story was told by Anjali to Anil,s family]

Anjali : This way I was killed . I hope Anil mom means Reema aunty has understood . So that's why I killed the people .

Reema Aunty : Ok . But the business man is left . You should kill him . Don't leave that monster .

Anjali : Ok

After that :

[Now the ghost went to kill the business man]

[In factory]

The ghost dim the lights and killed the securities .

When Rahul saw this from camera he took his remaining guards and started running from there . The ghost caught Rahul and locked in an room and killed him .

Anil I mean Anjali it took the village people to police station and told what exactly has happened . The police filed the case . The court also heard the Injustice .

Chief Justice : Anil but where is Rahul ??

Anil : I think ....

[Suddenly the ghost entered into Anil]

Anjali : Chief Justice I am Anjali the ghost who have killed all people . I have killed Rahul also . My son is in ashram he should be leaved from there. Handle him to my husband. Anil and his family don't know about this because they are new to village.

[Chief Justice was confused]

Chief Justice : So what we can do. ?

Anjali : As a ghost I wanted to tell you that my husband want bail . Because who killed me ;also killed them . My husband not did anything .

Chief Justice : Who is he ??

Anjali: He is Ram .

Chief Justice: Ram Kumar ??

Anjali: Yes .

[After that the court leaved Ram from court]

Anjali : Chief Justice the factory should be ban .

Chief justice : Ok .

[After 10 minutes]

Chief Justice : The court order is , that Ram should be left out.There is Anjali,s mistake to kill the people . The only reason why court not arrested anyone ,because Anjali is a ghost . The accust were also killed so they can't be arrested. The factory should be ban by government due to this reasons . The bungalow in village can be removed from haunted places list . Anyone can stay in that

Bungalow . The court can disperse.

[After Seeing Ram the ghost was happy and her soul got Rest & peace]

The END......

After that Ram Kumar took his child from Ashram.

Ram Kumar: Thank you Anil for your help.

Anil : It's my pleasure . Because I always support justice .

The Mystery was solved and the case also .

Story Written by : Mudliyar Uday Kumar .

Author Biography

I am an student of 13 years old of Scholar's English High School (Bhiwandi). If you have not read my first book i.e A great advocate " Kavin " go and read it . By purchasing the book on amazon or flipkart you can read it . Its price is rupees 98 only . I hope you liked this story .

Contents

Printed by Libri Plureos GmbH in Hamburg,
Germany